LEVEL 3 KRULIK

Krulik, Nancy E.   OCT 27 2018

Give a bot a bone

Give a 'Bot a Bone

Nancy Krulik and Amanda Burwasser

Give a 'Bot a Bone

Illustrated by Mike Moran

Sky Pony Press
New York

First Edition

While this book aims to accurately describe the steps a child should able to perform reasonably independently when cooking, a supervising adult should be present at all times. The authors, illustrator, and publisher take no responsibility for any injury cause while making a project from this book.

This is a work of fiction. Names, characters, places, and incidents are from the authors' imaginations and used fictitiously.

Sky Pony Press books may be purchased in bulk at special discounts for sales promotion, corporate gifts, fund-raising, or educational purposes. Special editions can also be created to specifications. For details, contact the Special Sales Department, Sky Pony Press, 307 West 36th Street, 11th Floor, New York, NY 10018 or info@skyhorsepublishing.com.

Sky Pony® is a registered trademark of Skyhorse Publishing, Inc.®, a Delaware corporation.

Visit our website at www.skyponypress.com.

www.realnancykrulik.com
www.mikemoran.net

10 9 8 7 6 5 4 3 2 1

Library of Congress Cataloging-in-Publication Data

Names: Krulik, Nancy E., author. | Burwasser, Amanda Elizabeth, author. | Moran, Mike, illustrator.
Title: Give a bot a bone / by Nancy Krulik and Amanda Burwasser ; Illustrated by Mike Moran.
Other titles: Give a robot a bone
Description: First edition. | New York : Sky Pony Press, Skyhorse Publishing, [2018] | Series: Project Droid ; #5 | Summary: Logan and Java need to make money fast, but none of their plans work out quite as they intended. |
Identifiers: LCCN 2017043704 (print) | LCCN 2017057184 (ebook) | ISBN 9781510726680 (eb) | ISBN 9781510726550 (pb : alk. paper) | ISBN 9781510726635 (hc : alk. paper) | ISBN 9781510726680 (ebook)
Subjects: | CYAC: Moneymaking projects—Fiction. | Robots—Fiction. | Humorous stories.
Classification: LCC PZ7.K9416 (ebook) | LCC PZ7.K9416 Giv 2018 (print) | DDC [Fic]—dc23
LC record available at https://lccn.loc.gov/2017043704

Cover illustration by Mike Moran
Cover design by Sammy Yuen

Printed in the United States of America

Interior design by Joshua Barnaby

For Emma Claire, the newest leaf on the family tree.

—NK and AB

To Lady, Isha, and Shadow, Moran's best friends.

—MM

CONTENTS

1. Rules, Schmools   1

2. Uh-Oh!   10

3. Must Dust   18

4. A Pretty (Lousy) Penny   26

5. Itchy, Itchy! Scratchy, Scratchy!   31

6. A Really Ruff Day   42

7. Where Wolf?   55

8. Bakin' Bacon   61

9. The Great Escape   69

10. The Toot Comes Out   85

Positively *Pawsome* Treats for You and Your Furry Friends   95

1.

Rules, Schmools

Plink. Plank. Plunk

Plink. Plank. Plunk.

I sat there listening to the raindrops hit our living room window.

Plink. Plank. Plunk.

Plink. Plank. Plunk.

Boy, do I hate rainy Saturdays. I had nothing to do except look in the mirror and count my eyelashes.

I was so bored.

My cousin, Java, wasn't bored though. He was busy playing with my mom's smartphone.

"Hey, Spike," my cousin asked the phone, "do you know what happened to the leopard that fell in the washing machine?"

"It came out spotless," Spike answered. "I've heard that one before."

Oh brother.

"I'm so tired of hanging around all day," I moaned.

Java's eyes opened wide.

He smiled excitedly.

And then he shouted, "**I can do it!**"

Java leaped up in the air and grabbed on to one of the blades of our ceiling fan.

"What are you doing?" I asked.

"I'm hanging around, too, " Java replied.

I watched Java spin around and around on the ceiling fan until I got dizzy.

"Get down from there," I ordered him. "You look ridiculous."

"Okay," Java said. He let go of the fan and landed on the ground with a loud *thud*.

"Shhh . . ." I warned. "Mom's taking a nap. Can't you hear her snoring through the door?"

"Of course I can hear her," Java said. "My supersonic ears can hear everything."

Java wasn't kidding. He really does have supersonic ears.

He also has eyes that can shoot laser beams.

And feet that can spring him up into the air like a rocket.

That's because Java isn't your typical third grade kid.

In fact, he isn't actually a kid at all. He's my android cousin.

My mom is a scientist. She likes to build things. So she built him.

My robot cousin's name is **J**acob **A**lexander **V**ictor **A**pplebaum. But I just call him Java.

Mom and I are the only ones who know that Java isn't a real kid. And we can't let anyone else know. That's because he's part of her secret scientific project: **Project Droid**.

The whole point of Project Droid is to figure out if an android can fit in with real people. So Java is programmed to do all sorts of real kid things.

"I meant, I just can't sit here being bored anymore," I explained. "I need to do something. There's got to be some place in this house we can play."

I thought for a minute. Maybe there

was a place.

"Let's go to the garage and kick around a soccer ball," I suggested.

Java shook his head. "Your mother's lab is in the garage," he said. "We are not allowed to be in there alone."

"We won't be alone," I told him. "I'll be there with you. And you'll be there with me. So neither of us would actually be alone."

Java stood there and thought about that for a minute. I could hear his hard drive ticking.

"That makes sense," he finally said.

I smiled as I ran up to my room to grab my soccer ball. At last, I was going to have some fun!

"Okay, I'll kick the ball to you, and you kick it back to me," I said to Java a few minutes later when we were in the garage.

I gave the ball my ultimate ninja kick.

It flew around Gunther, my mother's model skeleton.

It circled around her big barrel of beakers.

And then the soccer ball . . .

CRASH! CLANK! BOOM!

2.

Uh-Oh!

"Oh no!" I gasped. "This is bad. *Very* bad. Bad bad bad."

Java picked up the small metal machine that had fallen from a shelf.

"I think it is broken," he said as one of the blades fell to the ground.

He didn't seem upset about it at all. Then again, nothing upsets an android.

"Give me that," I said, snatching the metal machine from his hand. "Maybe I can pop that scissor blade back on."

I picked up the machine and tried to pop the piece back in place.

I twisted it.

I gave it a good shove.

And rammed it into place.

Yes! I had fixed it!

Clink. Clank. Clunk.

More pieces fell off.

"Is that what's supposed to happen?" Java asked.

Was he kidding me?

"No," I told him. "The blades are supposed to stay on."

"What kind of machine is that?" Java asked me.

"It's a Snip-De-Frizz," I told him. "Mom uses it to cut my hair. Or at least she used to. I don't think we're going to be able to fix it."

"Maybe your mother can fix it," Java suggested. "She is very good with machines."

I shook my head. "We can't let Mom know we broke this," I told him. "She can't find out we were in her lab alone."

"But we are not alone," Java reminded me. "I'm with you. And you're with me. Remember?"

"I remember. But for now, we should keep this our secret." I put the Snip-De-Frizz back on the shelf. "Let's get out of here before Mom finds us."

"What are you looking for, Logan?" Java asked as he watched me frantically scroll down the screen on my laptop.

"I need to find a store where I can buy a new Snip-De-Frizz," I told him, biting my lip nervously. "I'll replace the broken one before Mom finds out what happened." I scrolled a little faster. "Here it is. They sell it at Hairs and Stuff."

"That's not far," Java said. His motor began to whir. "I have downloaded the directions to my hard drive. You walk down Ishkabobble Avenue and turn right onto . . ."

"*Thirty-three dollars and seventy-seven cents?*" I shouted. "That hunk of junk costs *thirty-three dollars and seventy-seven cents?*"

Java peered over my shoulder at the website. "That is what it says."

"I don't have that kind of money." I whimpered. "What am I going to do? I can't just sweep this whole Snip-De-Frizz thing under the rug and forget about it."

Java gave me a strange look.

He smiled.

Then he shouted, "**I can do it!**"

The next thing I knew, my robot cousin was running back toward my mother's lab. He returned a minute later holding the Snip-De-Frizz.

What was he up to?

I watched as Java grabbed a broom from the closet. Then he put the Snip-De-Frizz on the floor, lifted the rug, and started sweeping.

"What are you doing?" I asked him.

"Sweeping this whole Snip-De-Frizz thing under the rug," he told me.

"That's not what I meant." I shook my head angrily. Sometimes, Java really grinds my gears.

Although this time . . .

"Thanks, Java!" I shouted, excited.

"You just gave me a great idea!"

3.

Must Dust

"Hello, mother dear," I said in my sweetest voice. Mom had just come downstairs after her nap. And Java and I were right there waiting for her.

"What do you want?" my mom asked.

"How do you know I want something?" I replied.

"Because you always want something

when you call me 'mother dear.'"

"Well, I don't want to ask you for an advance on my allowance. . . ." I said slowly.

"That's good," Mom said. "Because you aren't getting one. Why do you need money?"

Uh-oh. I didn't know how to answer that.

"It's . . . um . . . always good to have money," I said.

"That is true," Java agreed.

"So I was thinking, since I have nothing else to do, maybe I could do some chores to earn money," I told her.

"Well, I do have a few things around the house that could use a good cleaning," my mother agreed. "Okay. I will give you a list of chores. And I'll pay you when you've finished."

I didn't ask Mom how much she would pay me. No sense making her more curious than she already was.

Mom went to her desk and started to make a list of chores for Java and me:

Scrub the toilet
Unclog the drain under the kitchen sink
Put the books in ABC order
Dust the furniture
Vacuum the living room rug

Wow! That was a really long list.
I figured all that work had
to be worth at least thirty-
three dollars and seventy-
seven cents.

"Come on, Java," I said.
"We've got work to do."

"Okay, let's see what's next," I told Java a couple of hours later as I looked at the chores that were still left on Mom's list.

I had already scrubbed the toilet—which was super gross.

Then I pulled nasty ooey-gooey stuff out of the drain under the kitchen sink. *Yuck.*

And Java and I had put the books in ABC order. That took us three hours. There are a lot of books in my house.

"Okay, let's split up the rest of the list," I told Java. "We'll get it done faster that way. And the sooner we get the money, the better."

"Sure, Logan," Java agreed. "You're the boss."

I liked the sound of that.

I went to closet and got out the vacuum. "I'll vacuum the rug," I said. "You dust the furniture."

Java gave me a big smile.

He wiggled his ears.

And twitched his nose.

Then he shouted out, "**I can do it!**"

The next thing I knew, Java had popped open the vacuum bag. He was throwing dirty gray vacuum dust all over the place!

On top of the couch.

Under the chair.

All over the table.

Everywhere.

Cough cough. "What are you doing?" I asked Java as I tried to breathe under all that dust. *Cough. Cough.*

"I am dusting the furniture," Java replied. "Look how nice and dusty everything is now."

"What do you mean *nice* and dusty?" I shouted. *Cough cough.* "This isn't *nice* at all. You just wrecked the whole room. Now I have to vacuum even more."

Java gave me a funny look. I could tell he didn't understand what he had done wrong.

And I didn't feel like explaining it to him.

"How about you double-check that all the books are in the right order," I said. "I'll clean up the rest of the living room."

"Okay, Logan," Java said. "I will do whatever you say."

I looked around at the dust-covered couch, chair, and table.

"I know," I muttered. "That's the problem."

4.

A Pretty (Lousy) Penny

"You boys did a great job!" my mother said five hours later as she inspected the dusted—and re-dusted—living room.

She reached into her pocket.

I smiled. *Here comes the cash,* I thought.

All the scrubbing and dusting and ABC-ing was about to pay off. Any minute now, I would have the money I needed to buy a new Snip-De-Frizz. I might even have a little left over to buy a new deck of magic cards.

Mom opened her wallet. "I think all this work is worth two dollars," she said. She handed me two one-dollar bills.

I stared at the money in my hand. I couldn't believe it.

I know I should have said thank you, but the words wouldn't come out.

As mom walked out of the room, I shook my head.

"Two lousy dollars?" I grumbled. "That's all we get? For all that hard work?"

"Wait. There is more money, Logan!" Java exclaimed cheerfully.

I looked at him, curious. "There is?"

"Oh yes," Java assured me. "I found it under the couch cushions."

"Good job! How much did you find?"

Java reached into his pocket and pulled out . . .

A dime.

A nickel.

And two pennies.

"Seventeen cents?" I moaned. "That's no help at all."

"And I also found this," Java said, handing me an old red button.

I grabbed the button from his hand and angrily threw it on the floor.

"We're never going to get enough money to buy a new Snip-De-Frizz now," I whined. "Not when all we have so far is two dollars and seventeen cents."

"We also have a button," Java reminded me. "Don't forget the button."

5.

Itchy, Itchy! Scratchy, Scratchy!

"What are you doing, Logan?" Java asked me later that afternoon.

My cousin and I were in my room. I was busy arranging my toys by color into piles. Java was staring into space.

"What does it look like I'm doing?" I replied.

"I do not know," Java told me. "That is why I asked you."

"I'm going through my toys to see what I don't mind getting rid of," I explained. "Selling my toys is the only way I can think of to make the thirty-three dollars and seventy-seven cents quickly."

"But you do not need the thirty-three dollars and seventy-seven cents anymore," Java said.

I gave him a funny look. "I don't?" I asked him.

Java shook his big, goofy robot head. "No. You need thirty-one dollars and sixty cents. You already have two dollars, seventeen cents, and a red button."

Oh brother. Now Java was really pushing *my* buttons.

"That's still a lot of money we need," I told him. "And we have to get it fast. My hair doesn't shrink, you know. Sooner or later, Mom is going to want to cut it."

I pulled my old jack-in-the-box out of my toy chest. I started to turn the crank. The music began to play.

> *All around the mulberry bush*
> *the monkey chased the weasel.*
> *The monkey thought . . .*

POP!

The jack-*in*-the-box popped up so hard that the whole box flew out of

my hands.

"I guess I can call it a flying jack-in-the-box," I told Java. "People would pay a lot of money for that."

I reached into the toy chest and pulled out an action figure.

"It's only missing one arm," I said. "No one will notice."

"Do humans *like* old, broken toys?" Java asked me.

"Sure," I said, trying to sound really confident. "People buy old things all the time. You should see the kind of stuff they sell at flea markets."

"You are going to have a flea market, too?" Java asked me.

"Yep," I told him. "Tomorrow. In the park."

"I will help you, Logan," Java said. "I always want to help you."

"Get your toys here!" I called to the people passing through the park early Sunday morning. "Big toys. Little toys. Toys with one or two arms."

I had set up my flea market table near the big pond. It was sunny out—but it wasn't too hot. It seemed like every kid in town was outside playing.

Some were throwing balls around.

Others were going down the slides and pumping on the swings in the playground.

Still others were playing Frisbee with their dogs.

A schnauzer came over and grabbed my old stuffed bear that was missing an ear and started carrying it away in its mouth.

"That will be twenty dollars," I told him.

The schnauzer dropped the bear on the ground and ran back toward the path.

Just then, my best friend Stanley rode over on his bike. He hopped off and pet the schnauzer on the head.

"What are you doing?" Stanley asked me.

I looked at him. "Why does everyone keep asking me that?" I replied. "I'm selling my toys."

"Why?" Stanley asked me.

Before I could tell him about the broken Snip-De-Frizz, Java came racing over to my table. At least, I *thought* it was Java. It was hard to tell. He was running so fast he just looked like a big blurry blob.

"Hello, Logan," he said.

"Where have you been?" I asked him.

"I was finding fleas," he replied. "They are not so easy to find. Fleas are very tiny."

"You were finding *what*?" I asked.

"Fleas," Java repeated. He held up a shoebox with some pinholes poked in the top to let in air.

"Why would you want to *find* fleas?" I asked him.

"We are having a flea market," Java said, "so we need fleas to sell."

"You want us to sell fleas?" I asked him. "We can't do that."

"Why not?" Java asked. "These fleas are nice and juicy. I bet we can get ten cents apiece for them." He opened the box. "See?"

I looked in the box. "There's nothing in there."

"That can't be," Java said. He looked in the box, too. Then he shook his head. "I put them in there. Where could they have gone?"

I looked across the table. A fuzzy sheepdog was scratching behind his ears. A beagle was itching his belly. The schnauzer who had bit my teddy bear was spinning around on his butt trying to scratch an itch.

An itch that was probably caused by an escaped flea.

"I think I know where those fleas went," I told Java.

I looked at the dog owners. They did

not seem happy.

But I was thrilled.

A light bulb had just gone off in my head. Well, not a real light bulb. *I'm* not a robot. But I did get a great idea. I knew exactly how I was going to earn enough money to buy a new Snip-De-Frizz.

"Java," I exclaimed. "You're a genius!"

Java nodded. "That is how I was programmed," he said.

6.

A Really Ruff Day

"Please try to keep Pooky away from other dogs," Sherry said as she handed me her poodle's leash after school on Friday afternoon.

"We don't want her hanging around any mutt that could have fleas," Jerry added. "I heard a lot of dogs got fleas in the park last weekend."

"You're looking pretty shaggy there, Logan," Sherry said. "Are you sure *you* don't have fleas?"

I ran my hand through my hair. It had been almost a week since I'd broken Mom's Snip-De-Frizz. My bangs *were* definitely getting shaggy. I didn't need Sherry to tell me that.

Still, I gave her a phony smile. "Pooky will not get fleas at the Pampered Puppy

Palace," I assured the Silverspoon Twins.

I was trying to be nice to the Silverspoons. A guy's *got* to be nice to his customers. And for now, Jerry and Sherry were my customers.

Because the Pampered Puppy Palace was my new business.

All week long, Java and I had been handing out flyers to everyone we saw— well, at least everyone who had a dog.

Big dogs.

Little dogs.

Hairy dogs.

Smelly dogs.

It turned out, a lot of people in town had dogs that needed to be cleaned and walked. And those dogs were all in my

44

backyard, ready for a good grooming.

We already had ten customers!

"Now you're sure you know how to bathe dogs, right?" Sherry asked me.

"Of course," I told her. "I've been doing it for years."

That was a lie. I had never bathed a dog in my life.

I didn't have a dog.

In fact, I had never had a pet before—unless you counted the garden slug I found once. I named him Puddles. But he wasn't much fun.

I was actually *afraid* to ask my mom for a real pet now. Look what happened when I asked her for a brother. She built me a robot cousin instead.

At the moment, that cousin, Java, was hanging out with some of the dogs—and *scratching behind his ear. With his foot.* Which was strange. I didn't think robots could get itchy.

"Be careful when you walk Pooky," Jerry told me. "She pulls a little."

Sherry giggled. "Yeah. Just a little."

I looked at Pooky. She wasn't a big dog. How hard could she pull?

"Okay, we'll see you later," Jerry said. He and Sherry turned to leave.

"Yep," I called to the twins. "See you—"

WHOA!

The next thing I knew, Pooky was pulling me across the lawn on my belly.

For a little dog, she sure was strong. At least, too strong for me.

But not too strong for a *droid*!

"Hey, Java!" I called. "Can you come here and hold on to Pooky? I have to fill the bucket with flea shampoo."

"You are going to shampoo fleas?" Java asked as he walked toward me. "I thought we were going to wash the *dogs*."

I didn't even bother trying to explain it to him. I had too much to do.

I began filling the giant bucket I'd borrowed from my mom's lab with shampoo and water.

I made sure to keep the tub of water far away from Java. He can't get wet. If he does, his battery will short-circuit. I'd already seen that happen, and I didn't want a repeat.

Before I could finish filling the bucket, a Great Dane and a Chihuahua came running over. They knocked the bucket on its side.

Soapy water spilled all over my pants and my brand-new sneakers.

The grass around me turned all muddy and slippery.

"Whoops!" I shouted as I tripped, trying to reach for the Great Dane. "Come back here, Tiny!"

The hose I was using to fill the bucket

was spraying water everywhere. The dogs started running in circles, trying to get away from the water.

But I wasn't worried about the dogs.

"Java, get out of here before you get wet!" I shouted.

Luckily, Java did as he was told.

Exactly the way I meant it.

For once.

Three hours later . . .

All the dogs were washed and flea-free. Now all that was left to do was dry them.

"Hey, Java!" I called to my cousin. "Can you blow-dry the dogs?"

Java smiled.

He took a deep breath. Well, it looked like he did, anyway. Droids don't actually breathe.

And then he shouted out, **"I can do it!"**

WHOOOOOOOOSH!

The next thing I knew, Java was blowing the dogs dry—with his mouth.

Only he wasn't just blowing a light warm breeze like a hair dryer would.

He was blowing hard . . . like a *hurricane!*

The Java-strength winds were blowing the dogs all around our yard.

"STOP!" I shouted to Java. "Stop blowing!"

Java stopped blowing. And so did the wind.

Thump.

Bump.

Kerplump.

The dogs all fell to the ground. They stared up at me.

I stared down at them.

They were filthy. Every one of them was covered in leaves and mud. Pooky even had a bird's nest on her head.

No customer would ever pay to have his dog look like that.

And it was too late to give them each another bath.

Which meant that, thanks to Java, I had done all that work for nothing.

Again.

7.

Where Wolf?

"Nice hair, Logan." Sherry Silverspoon said with a laugh as I climbed the steps onto the bus on Monday morning.

"It looks even worse than Pooky's hair did after you bathed her," Jerry added. "All that's missing is the bird's nest."

"My mom has to take Pooky to a real groomer today," Sherry told me. "Dad said we should make you pay for it."

I gulped. I didn't know how much a real groomer cost, but I bet it was more than the two dollars and seventeen cents I had saved up.

"Mom talked him out of it though," Sherry continued.

Phew.

"Hey," Stanley whispered in my ear, "here she comes."

Without even looking, I knew who Stanley meant. Nadine Vardez had just gotten on the bus.

I moved over in my seat to make room.

I sat up tall.

I smiled at her.

Please sit here. Please sit here, I thought

to myself.

But Nadine stopped where Java was sitting, and sat down next to him.

"How are you doing, Java?" Nadine asked him.

"My gears are all oiled and none of my wires are crossed," Java told her.

Nadine gave him a funny look.

"You know my cousin," I said quickly. "He has a funny way of talking." I laughed really hard.

"You're hilarious," Nadine told Java.

"And he's got a nice haircut," Sherry pointed out. "Not like his werewolf cousin over there."

I frowned. Sure, Java's hair was perfect. Robot hair doesn't grow. But of course I couldn't say that.

"You better not get too close to Logan, Stanley," Jerry warned my best friend. "I heard somewhere that werewolves eat kids."

"*Arooo!*" Sherry howled, trying to sound like a werewolf.

"*Arooooooo!*" Jerry echoed.

"Don't let those two make you feel bad," Stanley told me. "I've seen pictures of my dad when he was in high school. His hair was wild. My mom thought it was cool."

I slumped down in my seat. The last person I wanted to look like was Stanley's dad. Or anybody's dad.

I really needed a haircut. But I couldn't ask my mom to give me one.

Not until I earned enough money to buy a new Snip-De-Frizz.

And since I had no idea how I was going to do that, I was going to have to get used to all that howling.

"*Arooooooo!*"

8.

Bakin' Bacon

"Why don't we ever have any decent snacks around here!" I shouted angrily as I stomped through the kitchen slamming the cabinet doors.

It had been a rotten day.

No, not just rotten. *Super colossal* rotten.

I had been so busy trying to earn the

money to buy the Snip-De-Frizz that I'd forgotten to do my social studies homework over the weekend.

I missed the free throw in our basketball game during gym class.

And I spilled milk all over my pants during lunch. Boy, did that stink by three o'clock.

Right now, all I wanted was a giant stack of cookies and a glass of chocolate milk. But all we had in the fridge was some liver and onions from last night's dinner, a salmon and soybean salad, leftover meatloaf, and lots and lots of broccoli.

It's not easy having a scientist for a mother. She's always trying to fill me with brain food.

I didn't want brain food.

I wanted junk.

"What is wrong, Logan?" Java asked me.

"Those Silverspoons put me in a bad mood," I explained. "They're really mean. And spoiled. *They* wouldn't have to work this hard to make money. *They* would just open their piggy banks. For them, this would be a piece of cake!"

Java gave me a funny smile.

His eyes bounced up and down in his face.

Then he yelled out, "**I can do it!**"

The next thing I knew, Java had opened the refrigerator door. He stood there for a minute, staring at all the food.

Then he said, "We do not have a piece of cake," he said. "Will a piece of meatloaf do?"

I shook my head.

"We could bake a cake," Java said. "And then you could have a piece."

I thought about that for a minute.

Bake a cake. Bake a cake. Bake a . . .

"Java" I shouted, "you're a genius!"

Java gave me a funny look. "Why do you keep yelling that?" he asked.

I didn't answer him. Instead, I asked, "Java, do you have a recipe for chocolate chip cookies in your hard drive?"

I heard the hard drive in Java's belly begin to whir. Then he said, "You will need, flour, eggs, butter . . ."

As Java rattled off the ingredients, I ran around the kitchen grabbing each item and laying it out on the counter.

"And chocolate chips," Java added, finishing the list.

I looked in the cabinet. No chocolate chips.

"That stinks!" I said. "How are we supposed to make chocolate chip cookies without any chocolate chips?"

Java peered into the freezer. "There are bacon bits," he said. "Would those work?"

I thought for a minute. "Everybody likes bacon," I said. "It could be interesting. Like a secret ingredient that only our cookies have."

"Are you going to bake cookies now, Logan?" Java asked me.

Sometimes Java isn't as smart as he thinks he is. Why else would I have pulled out all those ingredients?

"Yes," I told him.

"Can my friends and I help?" Java asked.

"Your friends?" I looked around the kitchen. "What friends?"

"Well, you've already looked inside Chilly," he said.

I was pretty sure he meant the refrigerator.

"And we will definitely need Mixy to stir the ingredients," Java continued. "And when we clean up, Dishy-Washy will know just what to do."

I had forgotten that Java's best friends were our kitchen appliances.

"Sure," I told him. "You and your friends can help bake the cookies."

9.

The Great Escape

"This is the perfect spot!" I said excitedly as I laid out our plates of our bacon chip cookies Tuesday afternoon after school.

I had set up our bake sale table on Persnickety Plaza, right between the Lights, Camera, Action movie theater and Mr. Waggz's Pet Shop.

"People love to eat snacks at the movies," I explained to Java. "They will buy lots of cookies."

"That is a very smart idea, Logan," Java said.

I smiled proudly. It feels good when a genius robot calls you smart.

Just then, a group of teenage kids came walking toward us.

"Get your cookies here," I shouted loudly. "Fresh baked cookies."

"Did you make these?" one of the teenagers asked me.

I nodded. "My cousin and I baked them all by ourselves," I said proudly.

"Well, not *all* by ourselves," Java corrected me. "My friends helped, too. Remember, Mixy stirred the batter and . . ."

I clapped my hand over Java's mouth

before he could name any more of his kitchen appliance buddies.

"We even came up with a secret recipe," I told the kids. "Try them. They're fifty cents apiece."

"That's cheaper than snacks at the movies," one guy said. He handed me a dollar. "I'll take two."

"Me, too." His pal handed me another a dollar.

"I'll take three," their friend said. He handed me a dollar and two quarters. I gave him three cookies.

The first guy took a bite of one of his cookies. He started to chew.

I stood up tall, waiting for him to say how yummy they were. And to ask what the special ingredient was—which I would never tell him. It was a secret after all.

The guy chewed a little more. He swallowed. And then he made an awful face.

"That's disgusting," he told me. "What did you put in those things?"

"Baco—" Java said.

I clapped my hand over his mouth. "It's a secret, remember?"

Java nodded.

"I want my money back," the guy said, throwing his other cookie on the ground angrily.

"Me, too," his friend said.

"Me, three," the other kid said.

I shook my head. "No backsies," I said. "You buy it, you own it."

The three teenagers glared at me. My knees started to shake. My heart started to pound. A big glob of sweat formed under my nose.

But I wasn't giving them back any money.

"Let's go, you guys," one of them finally said. "We're going to miss the movie."

As my first customers walked away, I shrugged. "Clearly they have no taste," I told Java.

"They might," Java replied. He reached over and licked my face.

"What are you doing?" I asked him.

"Seeing what a human tastes like," Java said. "My electronic taste buds are registering salt. And a little ketchup from yesterday's french fries. Did you forget to wash your face, Logan?"

"Get off of me," I grumbled. "That's not what I meant by taste!"

I picked up one of the cookies.

I took a bite.

And then I spit it out.

"These are awful!" I exclaimed. "I probably should have tasted them before I started selling them. No one is going to want to eat these things."

I frowned and pushed my hair out of my eyes. Another money idea ruined.

Just then, a woman with two of the biggest dogs I've ever seen walked past my table. She was trying to pull her dogs into Mr.Waggz's Pet Shop.

But the pooches had something else in mind. They pulled her straight toward our bake sale table.

Chomp! Chomp! Chomp!

It took only two seconds for the big dogs to gulp down the cookies the teenagers had tossed on the ground.

"Oh no!" the dogs' owner cried. "Please tell me those aren't chocolate chip cookies."

"They're not," I assured her.

"They're bacon chip cookies," Java said.

"Bacon chips?" the woman repeated. "No wonder my dog gobbled them down. Samson and Charlie love bacon. How much are the dog treats?"

"Those are not dog treats," Java said. "They are . . ."

"*Gourmet* dog treats," I said quickly, before Java could finish his sentence.

"And they are all homemade. Only fifty cents apiece."

"I'll take ten," the dog owner said.

She handed me a five-dollar bill.

"Thank you," I said. "And here are your cookies. Um . . . er . . . I mean your *dog treats*."

As the woman and her dogs walked away, I started shouting again. "Get your dog treats! Homemade dog treats here."

Another dog owner walked over to our bake sale table. His puppy started barking and jumping up and down excitedly.

"I think King Kong wants a treat," the owner said.

I handed the man a dog treat and said,

"That will be fifty cents please."

But before he could hand me the money, King Kong leaped up and grabbed another treat from the table.

"Now, that will be a dollar," I said.

As King Kong and his owner walked off, I smiled happily at Java. "This is amazing! I told him. "Our secret recipe is going to make us the dog food kings! We've opened the door to a whole new business!"

Java smiled back at me.

He licked his lips.

And tapped his toes.

Then he shouted out, **"I can do it!"**

The next thing I knew, Java had run to Mr. Waggz's Pet Shop and flung open the door.

"Hey, everybody! Come see our new business!" he shouted. "The door is open!"

There were a few dogs with their owners inside the pet shop.

At least they were inside *before* Java opened the door.

The minute those pooches caught a whiff of our bacon chip treats, they were pulling on their leashes, trying to get to our bake sale.

One of the dogs pulled so hard, he knocked over a cage full of little white mice.

The mice spilled out of the cage and started running all over the pet shop.

They hid in the corners.

They climbed up the walls.

And a whole crew of them escaped out the front door.

Mr. Waggz was *not* happy!

"Look what you've done!" he shouted angrily at Java.

"I did not do anything," Java replied calmly. "That Neopolitan Mastiff knocked over the cage."

Mr. Waggz's face turned beet red. For a minute, I thought his eyes were going to burst out of his head.

"Catch them!" he ordered Java. "Catch my mice!"

Java just stood there for a minute staring at the little white mice. Then he went into action, scooping up the mice at record speed.

I went into action, too. Only I wasn't scooping up mice. I was scooping up *cash!*

"Fifty cents a treat," I called out to the stampeding dogs and their owners. "Come and get 'em!"

10.

The Toot Comes Out

"It was really nice of Mr. Waggz to buy up the rest of our treats," I told Java later that afternoon.

"It was even nicer of him to say he would pay us just to go away," Java said. "I did not know that going away was a job humans could get paid for."

"I'm just glad we were able to afford a new Snip-De-Frizz," I told Java. "I don't want to toot my own horn, but it was pretty smart of me to have that bake sale."

Java's eye bugged out. A big smile formed on his face. **"I can do it!"** he shrieked.

His body spun around. He stuck his rear end in the air. And he let out a giant *TOOOOOT!*

I laughed. At least it didn't smell.

"Can I try the Snip-De-Frizz, Logan?" Java asked me.

I wiped my bangs off my forehead. I figured Java probably had some hair-cutting program in his hard drive. After all, Mom had thought of everything else.

"Just be careful," I said, handing him the Snip-De-Frizz. "All you do is push the . . ."

Buzzzzz . . .

I never finished the sentence. Java was already snipping away at my head. A moment later, he stopped and looked at me proudly.

"All finished," he said. "Take a look."

I got up to look in the mirror of my mom's Magneto Reflecto 9000.

"AAAAAAAAAHHHHHHH!"

I couldn't believe my eyes. I was bald.

Completely bald.

Bald.

Bald.

Bald.

"*AAAAAHHHHHHH!*" I screamed again.

Mom came running into the lab.

"Logan! What are you doing in here? You know the rule . . ." Mom stopped suddenly and stared at me. "What did you do to your head? You look like an ostrich egg."

"*I* didn't do it. Java did," I told her. "He shaved my whole head with the Snip-De-Frizz."

"Impossible," Mom said. "That thing's been broken for over a month."

What?

That meant *I* hadn't broken it after all.

But I couldn't tell Mom that. I didn't want her to know that this wasn't the first time I had been in her lab without her.

"It's a miracle!" I said. "The Snip-De-Frizz fixed itself!"

"No it didn't," Java blurted out. "That's a new Snip-De-Frizz. Remember, Logan? We broke the old one."

Mom gave me an angry look. Thanks to my big-mouthed, tattletale of an android cousin, I was in trouble.

"Normally, you'd be grounded for three weeks for going in my lab without me," Mom said. "But I think looking like a bald eagle for a couple of weeks is punishment enough."

I took another look in the Magneto Reflecto 9000. Mom wasn't kidding. Wait until the Silverspoons got a look at my shiny, round head. They were never

going to let me forget this.

Java stared at me. He looked around the lab.

Finally, he grabbed a baseball cap off Gunther the skeleton's head, and handed it to me.

"This is kind of like hair, Logan!" Java beamed. "Put it on."

I put the cap on my head and stared at my reflection.

I did look sort of cool.

Java smiled broadly. He seemed really proud of himself.

I had to laugh.

Sometimes it's hard to stay mad at an android cousin.

Positively Pawsome Treats for You and Your Furry Friends

Logan's cookie recipe wasn't something humans wanted to sink their teeth into. But the dogs sure loved them.

Turn the page for a recipe you can actually share with your dog.

You will both find them positively *pawsome!*

Here's What You Will Need

- 1 banana, sliced thinly
- Juice of 1 lemon
- 2 tablespoons of butter, melted
- 2 tablespoons brown sugar
- 1 cup chunky peanut butter
- ½ cup honey (Only for adult dogs. If you have a puppy, leave out the honey. The treats will still be yummy.)
- 1 cup flour
- Mixing bowl
- Baking Sheet
- Parchment paper
- Pastry brush
- 1 handy-dandy adult helper

Handy-Dandy Adult Helper

Banana

Honey

Lemon

Flour

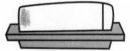

Butter

Mixing Bowl

Brown Sugar

Baking Sheet

Peanut Butter

Parchment Paper

Pastry Brush

Here's What You Do:

1 Ask your
handy-dandy
adult helper to
preheat your oven
to 350 degrees.

2 Place the bananas
in the mixing bowl.
Squeeze the lemon
juice over the
bananas to make
sure they don't
turn brown.

3 Place a sheet of parchment paper on the baking sheet. Use a pastry brush to cover the parchment paper with one tablespoon of melted butter.

4 Sprinkle one tablespoon of sugar over the melted butter.

5 Lay out the banana slices evenly on the baking sheet.

6

Brush the banana slices with the remaining butter and sprinkle with the remaining sugar.

7

Have an adult place the banana slices in the oven and allow them to bake until they are golden brown. (About one hour).

8

Set the banana slices aside to cool.

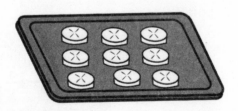

9 While the bananas are cooling, mix the peanut butter and honey together.

10 Stir the flour into the peanut butter and honey mixture.

11 Mix in the baked bananas.

12 Line the baking sheet with a fresh piece of parchment paper.

13 Drop tablespoon-sized clusters of the mixture onto the baking sheet.

Have an adult place the cookies in the oven and allow them to bake for 20 minutes, or until they are golden brown.

Let the cookies cool completely before you and your furry friend take a bite.

(If you have any questions about giving your dog, or any other dog, treats please have your handy-dandy grown-up assistant call a veterinarian for advice.)

About the Authors

Nancy Krulik is the author of more than two hundred books for children and young adults including three *New York Times* bestsellers and the popular Katie Kazoo, Switcheroo; George Brown, Class Clown, and Magic Bone series. She lives in New York City with her husband and a crazy beagle mix. Visit her online at www.realnancykrulik.com.

Amanda Burwasser holds a BFA with honor from Pratt Institute in New York City. Her senior thesis earned her the coveted Pratt Circle Award. A preschool teacher, she resides in Forestville, California.

About the Illustrator

Mike Moran is a dad, husband, and illustrator. His illustrations can be seen in children's books, animation, magazines, games, World Series programs, and more. He lives in Florham Park, New Jersey. Visit him online at www.mikemoran.net.